cutie mar[k] [c]re[w]

COLLECTOR'S GUIDE

Contents

Apple Bloom 2
Applejack 4
Baby Flurry Heart . 10
Big Mac 12
Cheerilee 14
Daring Do 16
DJ Pon-3 18
Flower Wishes 20
Fluttershy 22
Lily Valley 28
Lotus Blossom 30
Lyra Heartstrings . . 32
Maud Pie 34
. . . . 36
Photo Finish 38
Pinkie Pie 40
Princess Cadance . . 46
Princess Celestia . . 48
Princess Luna 50
Queen Chrysalis . . . 52
Rainbow Dash 54
Rarity 60
Royal Guard 66
Sand Bar 68
Sea Swirl 70
Shining Armor 72
Silverstream 74
Smolder 76
Spike 78
Spitfire 80
Starlight Glimmer . . 82
Sunset Shimmer . . . 84
Sweetie Drops 86
Trixie Lulamoon . . . 88
Twilight Sparkle . . . 90

fun studio INTERNATIONAL

Apple Bloom

"The Cutie Mark Crusaders will never be the same. We'll be better!"

A member of the trio known as the Cutie Mark Crusaders, APPLE BLOOM helps other ponies discover their special talents—and their cutie marks!

TYPE: Earth pony

HOME: Sweet Apple Acres, with Granny Smith, big sister (Applejack), and big brother (Big McIntosh)

BEST FRIENDS: Sweetie Belle and Scootaloo

BIGGEST WEAKNESS: Lets her ideas run away with her

SECRET HOBBY: Enjoys dancing

Fun Fact: Apple Bloom is learning potion making from Zecora the herbalist, a zebra who lives in the Everfree forest.

Release date: March 2019

Applejack

"We here at Sweet Apple Acres sure do like making new friends!"

A life of hard work has made APPLEJACK a little rough around the edges, but she's trustworthy and honest, and she's never afraid to tell it to you straight.

TYPE:	**Earth pony**
ELEMENT OF HARMONY:	**Honesty**
IT'S A FAMILY THING:	**Has a younger sister (Apple Bloom) and an older brother (Big McIntosh)**
TASTY TREATS:	**Her apple fritters are legendary in Ponyville**
FAVORITE ACTIVITY:	**A hard day's work**

Fun Fact: Applejack harvests her orchard by applebucking—clearing whole trees of apples with a single kick!

"You can't run away from your problems. Better to run to your friends and family."

Release date: June 2018

Release date: June 2018

Release date: October 2018

Release date: March 2019

Release date: June 2018

Release date: June 2018

Release date: October 2018

Release date: December 2018

Release date: March 2019

Release date: June 2018
Release date: October 2018
Release date: December 2018
Release date: March 2019

Baby Flurry Heart

Quote: None
(But give her time,
she's only a foal!)

Though she's just a little foal, FLURRY HEART's massive natural magical talent has caused big problems for her parents. Luckily, she's learning to control her powers.

TYPE: Alicorn pony

TINY BUT MIGHTY: Just one magical sneeze can blow through a ceiling

HER FAVORITE AUNT: Twilight Sparkle likes to foalsit when Cadance and Shining Armor need a break

A MYSTERY: Nopony knows why Flurry Heart was born an Alicorn—not even Princess Celestia

Fun Fact: Flurry Heart's crying once caused the Crystal Empire's Crystal Heart to shatter—luckily, it was restored by Twilight Sparkle and her friends.

Release date: December 2018

A pony of few words, BIG "MAC" MCINTOSH is the oldest of the Apple siblings. Like his younger sister Applejack, he's never afraid to lend a helping hoof.

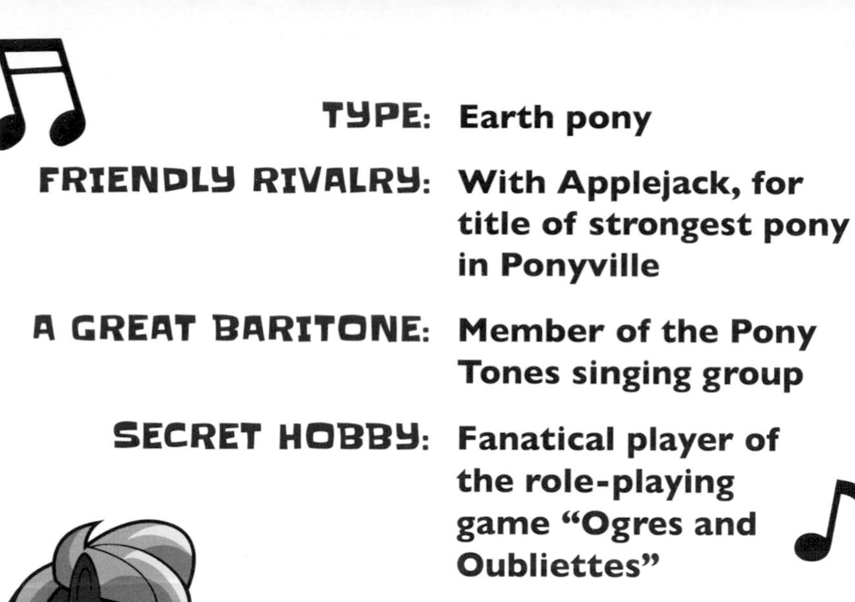

TYPE: Earth pony

FRIENDLY RIVALRY: With Applejack, for title of strongest pony in Ponyville

A GREAT BARITONE: Member of the Pony Tones singing group

SECRET HOBBY: Fanatical player of the role-playing game "Ogres and Oubliettes"

SWEET ON: Sugar Belle from Our Town (they're dating!)

Fun Fact: He once disguised himself as a mare in order to participate in the Sisterhooves Social with Apple Bloom.

Release date: October 2018

Cheerilee

Kind and patient Miss CHEERILEE is the teacher at the Ponyville Schoolhouse. Her gentle guidance and enthusiasm for learning helps her students bloom.

TYPE: Earth pony (TV series), Pegasus pony (toy)

DREAMS ACHIEVED: Always wanted to be a teacher

FIRM BUT FAIR: Adores her students, but doesn't let them get away with misbehavior

NOTABLE GRADUATES: Former teacher of Scootaloo, Apple Bloom, and Sweetie Belle

Fun Fact: The Cutie Mark Crusaders once gave her a love potion, causing her to fall in love with Big Mac on Hearts and Hooves Day!

Release date: June 2018

A globe-trotting explorer, DARING DO poses as reclusive author A.K. Yearling to write about her real, exciting, and death-defying adventures.

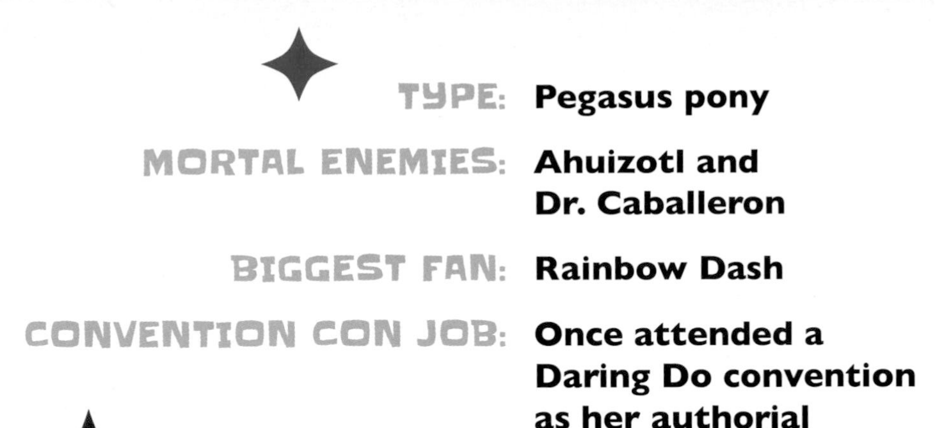

TYPE: Pegasus pony

MORTAL ENEMIES: Ahuizotl and Dr. Caballeron

BIGGEST FAN: Rainbow Dash

CONVENTION CON JOB: Once attended a Daring Do convention as her authorial alter ego

Fun Fact: She never keeps any of the treasures she recovers—instead, she donates them to museums for study.

Release date: March 2019

DJ Pon-3

DJ PON-3 is always at home behind the turntables, on call for whenever a party needs her special spinning skills.

TYPE: Unicorn pony

PARTY PONY: Present at every party with her turntables in tow

SIGNATURE LOOK: Rarely seen without her sunglasses and headphones

Release date: June 2018

Release date: October 2018

Release date: October 2018

Release date: December 2018

Flower Wishes

FLOWER WISHES helps her friends run the florists' shop in Ponyville, and enjoys gardening in her spare time.

TYPE: Earth pony

THREE OF A KIND: Best friends with Lily Valley and Rose

SIDE BUSINESS: Sometimes sells pots and pans in Ponyville's open-air marketplace

Fun Fact: Though her toy name is Flower Wishes, she is known as Daisy in the animated television series.

Release date: June 2018

Fluttershy

FLUTTERSHY opened an animal sanctuary for all kinds of creatures in need. Although she can be timid, her friends have taught her the courage to stand up

TYPE:	**Pegasus pony**
ELEMENT OF HARMONY:	**Kindness**
SECRET TALENT:	**Has a beautiful singing voice (but is too shy to perform in public)**
DID SOMEONE SAY PARTY?:	**Has weekly tea parties with Discord, her draconequus friend**
FAVORITE ACTIVITY:	**Talking to her animal friends**

Fun Fact: Fluttershy possesses a power over animals that her friends call "The Stare."

Release date: June 2018

"Sometimes you have to do things, even though you might fail."

Release date: October 2018

Release date: December 2018

Release date: March 2019

Release date: March 2019

Release date: June 2018

Release date: June 2018

Release date: October 2018

Release date: December 2018

Release date: December 2018

Release date: March 2019

Release date: June 2018
Release date: June 2018
Release date: October 2018
Release date: October 2018
Release date: December 2018
Release date: March 2019

Lily Valley

LILY VALLEY is often in the company of her best friends, Flower Wishes and Rose. These three mares have a tendency to get over-excited, whether the occasion calls for it or not.

TYPE: Earth pony

HAS FREAKED OUT ABOUT: Equestria-threatening catastrophes

HAS ALSO FREAKED OUT ABOUT: A broken flower stem

Fun Fact: Lily Valley helps run Ponyville's flower shop.

Release date: March 2019

Lotus Blossom

One of the two ponies who works at the Ponyville Day Spa, LOTUS BLOSSOM specializes in massages, makeovers, mud baths, and other treatments to make everypony feel like their best self.

TYPE: Earth pony

OCCUPATION: Beautician

SPECIALTY TREATMENTS: Seaweed wraps and horn filing

Fun Fact: She's almost never seen without her friend and fellow spa pony, Aloe.

Release date: March 2019

"Anything's possible when you know somepony as well as we know each other!"

Although she tends to stick to the background, LYRA is almost never seen without her best friend

TYPE: Unicorn pony

STANDOUT MOMENT: Was a bridesmaid at Princess Cadance's wedding

PARTNERS IN JUSTICE: Later joins S.M.I.L.E. (Secret Monster Intelligence League of Equestria) as Sweetie Drops' partner

DARKEST SECRET: She once ate imported oats that Sweetie Drops had been saving for a special occasion

Fun Fact: She and Sweetie Drops are together almost all the time—see if you can spot them!

Release date: October 2018

Release date: March 2019

Maud Pie

MAUD is a stoic and soft-spoken pony with a love of geology. Though she and younger sister, Pinkie Pie, couldn't seem more different, they're the best of friends.

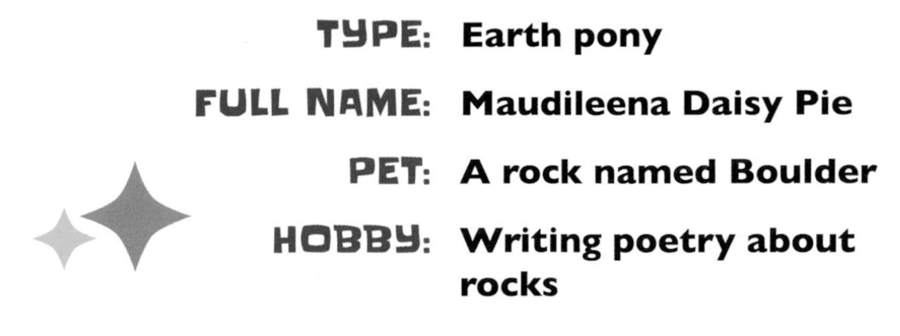

TYPE: Earth pony

FULL NAME: Maudileena Daisy Pie

PET: A rock named Boulder

HOBBY: Writing poetry about rocks

BIGGEST FAN: Pinkie Pie

Fun Fact: She once smashed a giant boulder to bits with her bare hooves to save Pinkie Pie from a rock slide.

Release date: December 2018

Well-meaning but a little klutzy, [muffin icon] is Ponyville's mail delivery mare. Although her absent-minded nature sometimes leads to mix-ups, she's loved by her fellow Ponyville citizens.

TYPE: Pegasus pony

BEST FRIEND: Dr. Hooves

COOL COSTUME: She sometimes wears a costume of paper bags for Nightmare Night

Fun Fact: Accidentally mixed up the date on the invitations for Cranky Doodle and Matilda's wedding.

Release date: June 2018

Release date: March 2019

Photo Finish

As Equestria's premiere fashion photographer, PHOTO FINISH is usually accompanied by a full entourage of assistants, and always makes a flashy entrance and exit.

TYPE: Earth pony

FAVORITE PHRASE: "I go!"

TRENDSETTER: Her attention can mean instant fame for ponies trying to make it in fashion

AN EYE FOR BEAUTY: Once photographed Rarity for the magazine *Vanity Mare*

Fun Fact: She once scouted Fluttershy as a model, making the shy Pegasus one of the most famous ponies in Equestria.

Release date: October 2018

PINKIE PIE is always ready with a joke, a song, or a silly dance to bring joy and cheer to anypony she meets. Nothing makes Pinkie Pie happier than seeing her friends happy, too!

TYPE:	**Earth pony**
ELEMENT OF HARMONY:	**Laughter**
FULL NAME:	**Pinkamina Diane Pie**
FAVORITE "ACCESSORY":	**Party cannon**
MMM, FREE CUPCAKES:	**Lives and works at Sugarcube Corner bakery**
IT'S A FAMILY THING:	**Has three sisters named Limestone, Marble, and Maud**

Fun Fact: Pinkie Pie grew up on a rock farm—not exactly Pinkie's idea of "fun." Her family may not always get her, but they always have her back!

Release date: June 2018

"My friends laugh with me, not at me."

Release date: June 2018

Release date: October 2018

Release date: December 2018

Release date: December 2018

Release date: March 2019

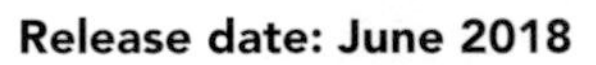

Release date: June 2018

Release date: June 2018

Release date: October 2018

Release date: October 2018

Release date: December 2018

Release date: March 2019

Release date: March 2019

Release date: June 2018
Release date: October 2018
Release date: December 2018
Release date: March 2019

Princess Cadance

A patient, kind, and devoted leader of the Crystal Empire, PRINCESS CADANCE's heart is always full of love for family, friends, and kingdom alike.

TYPE: Alicorn pony

FULL NAME: Princess Mi Amore Cadenza

THE PRINCESS OF LOVE: Powers stem from her love and empathy for others

IT'S A FAMILY THING: Mother to Alicorn Princess Flurry Heart and married to Twilight's brother, Shining Armor

Release date: June 2018

Release date: October 2018

Release date: December 2018

Princess Celestia

Equally capable of battling ancient evils and settling minor disputes, this magnificent pony is beloved by all her subjects.

TYPE: Alicorn pony

MAKES HER HOME IN: Canterlot Castle

UNDER HER WING: Twilight Sparkle's mentor and teacher

PRINCESS OF THE SUN: Controls the rising and setting of the sun each day

IT'S A FAMILY THING: Older sister to Princess Luna, who she once banished to the moon

Release date: June 2018

Release date: October 2018

Release date: December 2018

Princess Luna

"As Princess of the Night, it is my duty to protect your dreams."

PRINCESS LUNA **is Celestia's younger sister, and uses her powers to protect Equestria and rule over the night.**

TYPE: Alicorn pony

USED TO BE BAD: Spent one thousand years banished to the moon as Nightmare Moon

EXILE CAN BE HARD: She has had difficulty adjusting to modern pony life

PRINCESS OF THE MOON: Has power over the moon and stars

JUST FOR FUN: She enjoys playfully frightening foals on Nightmare Night

Fun Fact: Princess Luna can visit ponies' dreams, and helps guard against nightmares.

Release date: October 2018

Queen Chrysalis

A powerful and manipulative creature, QUEEN CHRYSALIS once ruled over the Changelings, a race of magical shapeshifters who feed on emotion.

TYPE: Changeling

MOST HUMILIATING DEFEAT: Dethroned in favor of King Thorax, the new Changeling leader

MOST EVIL DEED: Once took the form of Princess Cadance in an effort to take over Equestria

CURRENT TARGET OF HER VENGEANCE: Starlight Glimmer

Fun Fact: As a changeling, she can change her appearance to look like almost anything or anyone.

Release date: December 2018

Rainbow Dash

The daring pony known as RAINBOW DASH lives for action, adventure, and speed! Whenever there's excitement, that's where she'll be!

TYPE: Pegasus pony

ELEMENT OF HARMONY: Loyalty

AWESOME MOVES: Known for her spectacular Sonic Rainboom

FAVORITE DRINK: Sweet Apple Acres' Apple Cider

DAY JOB: Helping the other Pegasi control the weather

Fun Fact: Rainbow Dash is a member of The Wonderbolts, the most talented flyers in Equestria!

Release date: June 2018

"I'd never leave my friends hanging!"

Release date: June 2018

Release date: October 2018

Release date: October 2018

Release date: December 2018

Release date: March 2019

Release date: March 2019

Release date: June 2018

Release date: June 2018

Release date: October 2018

Release date: December 2018

Release date: March 2019

Release date: June 2018
Release date: October 2018
Release date: October 2018
Release date: December 2018
Release date: March 2019

A talented designer and seamstress, RARITY runs several high-fashion boutiques, but is never too busy to lend a friend a helping hoof.

TYPE:	**Unicorn pony**
ELEMENT OF HARMONY:	**Generosity**
IT'S A FAMILY THING:	**Older sister to Sweetie Belle**
PROUDEST FASHION MOMENT:	**Designed Princess Cadance's wedding dress**
FAVORITE ACTIVITY:	**A relaxing spa day**

Fun Fact: Rarity loves to mine the gems she uses in her fashions herself—only the best will do!

Release date: June 2018

Release date: June 2018

"I simply cannot let such a crime against fabulosity go uncorrected."

Release date: June 2018

Release date: October 2018

Release date: October 2018

Release date: December 2018

Release date: December 2018

Release date: March 2019

Release date: March 2019

Release date: June 2018

Release date: December 2018

Release date: December 2018

Release date: June 2018

Release date: October 2018

Release date: October 2018

Release date: December 2018

Release date: March 2019

Release date: March 2019

Tasked with guarding Canterlot Castle, as well as protecting all the pony princesses of Equestria, the ROYAL GUARDS are always on alert for dangerous threats.

TYPE: Earth ponies, Unicorn ponies, and Pegasus ponies

ON THE JOB: Two royal guards pull Princess Celestia's flying chariot and escort her wherever she goes

ALSO KNOWN AS: The E.U.P. Guard (Earth, Unicorn, and Pegasus)

Fun Fact: Shining Armor once served as the captain of the Canterlot Royal Guard.

Release date: December 2018

The most easygoing member of the new class at Twilight's School of Friendship, SAND BAR always knows what to say to soothe hurt feelings when his new friends' personalities clash.

TYPE: Earth pony

FAVORITE HOLIDAY: Hearth's Warming Eve

BIGGEST FEAR: Letting his friends down

Fun Fact: He played the part of legendary magician Star Swirl the Bearded in Twilight's school play.

Release date: March 2019

SEA SWIRL loves the ocean. Even though she's a citizen of landlocked Ponyville, she takes regular train rides to the seaside to indulge in her favorite pastime—whale watching!

TYPE: Unicorn pony

FAVORITE ACTIVITY: Swimming

NOT A ONE-TRICK PONY: Regularly plays at the Ponyville Bowling Alley

Fun Fact: She's attended the Grand Galloping Gala in Canterlot.

Release date: March 2019

SHINING ARMOR is Twilight Sparkle's older brother, as well as the captain of Canterlot's Royal Guard, Princess Cadance's husband, and father to little Flurry Heart.

TYPE: Unicorn pony

PRINCE CONSORT: Co-rules the Crystal Empire with Princess Cadance

STILL A GUARD AT HEART: Extremely protective of his wife and child

BIG BROTHER-BEST FRIEND FOREVER: His nickname for his little sis is "Twily"

EMBARRASSING SECRET: Gets very emotional at other ponies' weddings

Release date: June 2018

Release date: December 2018

Although now a member of the new class at Twilight Sparkle's School of Friendship, this outgoing Hippogriff still has a lot to learn about life on land.

TYPE: Hippogriff/Seapony

FAVORITE THING ABOUT LAND: Stairs!

SHAPESHIFTER: Can change between Hippogriff and Seapony forms at will

Fun Fact: She's the cousin of Princess Skystar, making her Seapony (and Hippogriff) royalty!

Release date: March 2019

Although she retains her tough and competitive dragon attitude, SMOLDER has begun to open her scaly heart to the magic of friendship, just like her classmates.

TYPE: Dragon

GOOD WITH ADVICE: Teaches Spike about the dangers of dragon molting

FAVORITE SCHOOL SPORT: Buckball

Fun Fact: She's (currently) the only dragon enrolled at Twilight Sparkle's Magical School of Friendship.

Release date: March 2019

SPIKE is in charge of keeping track of Twilight's busy schedule and passing messages between the princesses via his magical dragon breath.

TYPE: Dragon

WHERE'D HE COME FROM?: Hatched by Twilight Sparkle during her first magic exam

NOT-SO-SECRET SECRET: Has a big crush on Rarity

OUR HERO!: Once single-handedly saved the Crystal Empire

FAVORITE ACTIVITY: Reading comic books

Release date: June 2018

Release date: December 2018

Release date: March 2019

"Being the best should never come at the expense of our fellow ponies."

SPITFIRE's goal is always to work hard and do better, and she holds everyone else to her high standards—even when that means giving them some tough love.

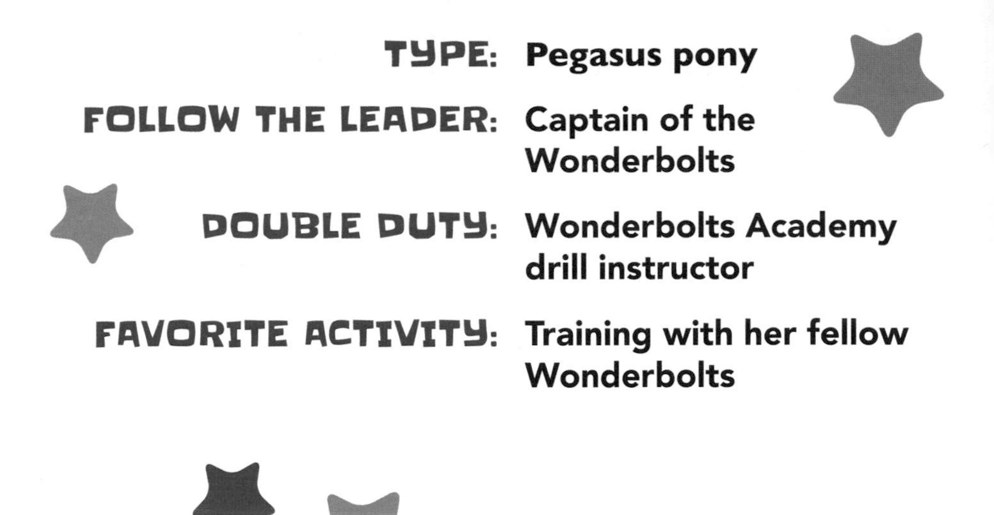

TYPE: Pegasus pony

FOLLOW THE LEADER: Captain of the Wonderbolts

DOUBLE DUTY: Wonderbolts Academy drill instructor

FAVORITE ACTIVITY: Training with her fellow Wonderbolts

Fun Fact: Rainbow Dash has saved her life, not once, but twice!

Release date: December 2018

Though she once used her magic to steal cutie marks from the Mane 6, STARLIGHT GLIMMER became Twilight Sparkle's first-ever friendship pupil.

TYPE: Unicorn pony

STRONGER THAN SHE SEEMS: Led the charge to dethrone the changeling queen, Chrysalis

LEARNING MAGIC: Studied with Sunburst, the Royal Crystaller, as a filly

BIGGEST WEAKNESS: Tends to act without thinking through her plans

CURRENT JOB: Guidance counselor at Twilight's Magical School of Friendship

Fun Fact: She once helped Princess Luna and Princess Celestia overcome their friendship problem by switching their cutie marks.

Release date: October 2018

Sunset Shimmer

"You can count on your friends to help you find the answers."

SUNSET SHIMMER attends high school, plays music—and occasionally battles otherworldly threats—with the other girls from Canterlot High.

TYPE: Unicorn Pony (turned human in *Equestria Girls*)

SHE'S IN THE BAND: Singer and rhythm guitarist of the Rainbooms

CAMPING OUT: Helped save Camp Everfree from evil forces

MAGICAL POWERS: Has the ability to sense other's feelings and memories through touch

Release date: June 2018

Release date: October 2018

Release date: December 2018

Release date: December 2018

Sweetie Drops

Often in the company of best friend Lyra Heartstrings, SWEETIE DROPS is content to live the quiet life of a Ponyville citizen—or so you'd think.

TYPE: Earth pony

ALIAS: "Bon Bon"

SECRET AGENT PONY: A former agent of the Secret Monster Intelligence League of Equestria (S.M.I.L.E.)

COVER STORY: Went undercover in Ponyville to leave her old life behind

Fun Fact:
She used to be a secret agent!

Release date: October 2018

Trixie Lulamoon

Once a travelling magician, TRIXIE LULAMOON had a tendency to cover her lack of actual magical talent with exaggerated bragging and theatrical flair.

TYPE: Unicorn pony

AN UNLIKELY PAIR: Good friends with Starlight Glimmer

FALSE ADVERTISING: Calls herself "The Great and Powerful Trixie"

USED TO BE BAD: Once took over Ponyville with the power of a stolen artifact

FAVORITE ACTIVITY: Performing in front of other ponies

Fun Fact: Although she isn't the best at real magic, Trixie is a very accomplished stage magician.

Release date: October 2018

Twilight Sparkle

"Friendship isn't always easy, but there's no doubt that it's worth fighting for."

A former student of the regal Princess Celestia, TWILIGHT SPARKLE started the School of Friendship where she teaches creatures throughout Equestria about the magic of friendship!

TYPE: Alicorn pony

ELEMENT OF HARMONY: Magic

FAVORITE THING TO DO: Read a good book

NO PLACE LIKE HOME: Lives in the Castle of Friendship

OLDEST FRIEND: Spike the Dragon

GOOD STUDENT: Loves to research ancient pony spells

Fun Fact: Was once a Unicorn—she changed into an Alicorn when she became a princess!

Release date: June 2018

"Reading is something everypony can enjoy, if they just give it a try."

2
Release date: October 2018
3
Release date: December 2018
3
Release date: December 2018
4
Release date: March 2019
4
Release date: March 2019

Release date: June 2018

Release date: June 2018

Release date: October 2018

Release date: December 2018

Release date: March 2019

Release date: June 2018

Release date: June 2018

Release date: December 2018

Release date: March 2019

Studio Fun International
An imprint of Printers Row Publishing Group
A division of Readerlink Distribution Services, LLC
10350 Barnes Canyon Road, Suite 100, San Diego, CA 92121
www.studiofun.com

Written by Rachael Upton
Illustrated by Hasbro
Designed by Jenna Riggs

Library of Congress Cataloging-in-Publication Data is available upon request.

Printers Row Publishing Group is a division of Readerlink Distribution Services, LLC.
Studio Fun International is a registered trademark of Readerlink Distribution Services, LLC.
All notations of errors or omissions should be addressed to Studio Fun International, Editorial Department, at the above address.

ISBN: 978-0-7944-4312-2

Manufactured, printed, and assembled in Shaoguan, China.

First printing, June 2019. SL/06/19

23 22 21 20 19 1 2 3 4 5